Disney's The Big Green

A Novel by J. J. GARDNER

Based on the Motion Picture from WALT DISNEY PICTURES
In Association with CARAVAN PICTURES
Executive Producer DENNIS BISHOP
Based on the Screenplay Written by HOLLY GOLDBERG SLOAN
Produced by ROGER BIRNBAUM
Directed by HOLLY GOLDBERG SLOAN

114 FIFTH AVENUE
NEW YORK, NY 10011-5690

Printed in the United States of America.
For information address Disney Press,
114 Fifth Avenue, New York, NY 10011-5690.

First Edition
1 3 5 7 9 10 8 6 4 2
Library of Congress Catalog Card Number: 95-69306
ISBN: 0-7868-4058-7

This book is set in 11.5-pt. Clarendon Light

Designed by Lara S. Demberg

TABLE OF CONTENTS

ELMA

The four boys, all aged thirteen, pedaled their bicycles down the dusty main street of Elma, Texas, population: 923. Not much was happening in Elma that day, but the boys knew that was not unusual. Not much ever happened in Elma anymore. Just about everybody who lived there agreed that Elma was the most boring town in Texas, especially if you were thirteen years old.

The boys rode slowly and lazily, until they reached the gas station and general store that was run by Polly's mom. They parked their bikes, laying them down in the weed patch beside the gas pump, and went inside. Polly's mother, who was counting the store inventory for the second time that day, was glad to see them. After all, they were the only customers she'd had all afternoon.

The boys stayed just long enough to buy a bag of cheese curls, then hurried back outside. One of them, Nick, kicked an empty beer can into the middle of Main Street, where it was immediately crushed by a passing truck.

"Two points!" Nick exclaimed.

Larry burst into an old song.

Jeffrey, who liked to think of himself as the leader of the group (though he wasn't) and liked to boss the others around (Larry in particular), said, "Change songs, Larry."

"I don't know any other songs," replied Larry.

Evan took up the rear. He always moved a little more slowly than the rest, probably because of his pants, which were always too long. While the other boys were climbing back onto their bicycles, Evan caught sight of an oddly shaped rock. Wow, he thought. He bent down and picked up the stone, and his thick-framed glasses slid down his nose.

"Hey, Evan?" asked Jeffrey. "How many rocks you got at home?"

"Lots," replied Evan as he studied the rock. "You know I collect them."

"What else is he gonna collect?" Nick shrugged. The others shrugged in agreement. After all, they lived in Elma.

And as everybody knew, Elma was the most boring town in Texas. In the world.

••••• •••••

The boys rode their bikes to a small two–room building that stood between two fields. The Elma schoolhouse served as both a high school and an elementary school. Mostly it was an embarrassment. On one side of the building was the recess yard and a baseball diamond that was covered with weeds. On the other side was another, larger field, also covered with weeds. A chain-link fence ran along the outside of this field, and two goalposts sagged at either end. A sign at the entrance proudly declared:

THE BIG GREEN
District 34 Recreation Area

The sign was so old and rusted, it was hard to read.

The boys laughed as they rode past the sign. There was nothing "big" about this field, and there was definitely nothing *green* about it.

The boys rode over to the recess field, dumped their bikes, and marched to the center of it. Nick handed the bag of cheese curls to Evan. Then Nick, Larry, and Jeffrey lay down on the ground.

Evan ripped open the bag and began sprinkling the cheese curls over his friends.

CRUNCH! Larry had snuck one of the cheese curls into his mouth.

"Larry!" chided Jeffrey.

"Just one!" explained Larry. "To see if they're fresh!"

"No more, Larry," warned Nick.

When Evan had finished covering his friends with chips, he lay down and sprinkled the rest of the bag on his own legs.

Then they waited. And waited. And waited.

Finally they saw a pigeon flying overhead. Soon the pigeon was joined by another pigeon, then another, and another. Now there were dozens of hungry pigeons circling overhead.

"Here they come," whispered Larry.

Suddenly the pigeons swooped down on the boys and began pecking and pulling greedily at the cheese curls that covered them. The boys laughed but tried to keep still.

No doubt about it, this was the most fun they had had all summer.

••••• •••••

Not far away, on the paved road that led toward the schoolhouse, three girls watched the boys disgustedly.

"I can't believe tomorrow we start another school year with those geeks," said thirteen–year–old Kate. She had a shag of unkempt hair and wore an outfit of rough-and-tumble clothes. In her hand was a pocketknife, her constant companion, that she was forever twirling absentmindedly like a baton.

"We've never gone to school with anyone but those geeks," added Sophia, who was a year younger than Kate.

"At least tomorrow we get a new teacher," said Polly, who was only eleven. She tagged behind her two friends, pulling her pet goat, Ernie, by a rope.

"Maybe," said Kate. "Maybe not. Nobody's shown up yet."

"I hope this year she won't drink," said Sophia.

"I hope she doesn't smell," said Polly.

"Mrs. Vancil smelled because of the medicine," said Sophia.

"I thought she smelled because she chewed garlic pills," said Kate.

"She smelled because she had such gross BO," Sophia suggested.

"She smelled because she chewed garlic pills, which she thought were medicine, which gave her gross BO," said Kate, making it official.

Sophia and Polly paused.

"I didn't know that," said Sophia.

"Me either," said Polly.

"The only thing we know for sure," added Kate, "is the new teacher will be a loser. Otherwise she wouldn't come here."

And with that, the three girls returned to their task at hand: namely, lining the road with a variety of crushable items, such as soda cans, a packet of mustard, and an empty milk carton. The idea was that a car passing by would flatten the stuff like a pancake. But the girls never stuck around to see the items get crushed anymore. It was just something to do.

••••• •••••

SCRUNCH! POP! HISS! SPLAT! The red convertible came to a screeching stop and the driver, a woman in her late twenties, got out and slammed the door.

"Oh, my God!" she shouted. Soda cans, milk cartons, and mustard was scattered and splattered over the road. But that wasn't what caused her to exclaim. In a field next to the school yard four boys were being attacked by dozens of pigeons!

The woman raced over to where the boys lay and looked around in a panic for something she could use to frighten away the birds.

She was in luck. There was a small toolshed nearby, and in front of it was a hose and spigot. She grabbed the hose, aimed it at the boys, and turned on the water full blast.

The startled pigeons took to the air in an explosion of flapping wings, and the woman was able to heave a sigh of relief. The four boys, though soaked, seemed unharmed. In fact, as they got to their feet she noticed that they seemed almost . . . angry.

"What're you doing?" snarled Jeffrey.

"I thought you were in trouble," answered the woman.

"So you hosed us?" asked Nick.

"I was trying to help," she insisted.

"Well, *thanks*!" snapped Jeffrey.

"I'm sorry," said the woman. "What *were* you doing?"

The boys gave her an "Isn't it obvious?" look.

"Feeding the birds," explained Evan as he tried shaking his water-soaked pants leg dry.

"There's not a lot to do around here," added Larry with a shrug.

"Who are you anyway?" Larry asked the woman.

"I'm the new teacher," replied the woman.

"No way!" the four boys exclaimed.

"Way," said the woman.

Way? The four boys exchanged bewildered expressions.

"What's she talking about?" Evan asked Nick.

"I'm here from England for a semester on a teaching exchange," the woman explained.

"Nobody tells us anything," said Jeffrey.

"There's two classes," began Nick. "Little kids—"

"And big kids," finished Jeffrey.

"I'm the teacher for the big kids," the woman told them.

"No way!" the four boys said again.

"Way," nodded the woman with a friendly smile. Then she added, "Hey, it's jolly good to meet you."

"*Jolly* good?" Nick repeated.

"The new teacher's a pirate," whispered Larry.

Sheriff Tom

Sheriff Tom Palmer sped down the road, the red light on top of his police car flashing. He had gotten a call about an emergency on Hicks Road that required his immediate attention.

Tom was glad to get the call. Not much police business that day, so Tom was anxious for some excitement. In fact, the last exciting thing Tom could remember happening in Elma was when big Sissy Whitehead got stuck in the doorway of her back porch. It took Tom, Cookie, and Ed to squeeze her out.

As he drove, Tom remembered how it was in Elma fifteen years earlier. That was back when everybody had jobs. Before the grain-processing plant closed. In those days Tom was the star quarterback for the Elma High School Armadillos. Of course, Elma had an actual high school back then. After the mill closed, most families moved away in search of jobs.

But Tom stayed on and became sheriff.

After a while Tom pulled over to the side of the highway and got out of his car. He had found the emergency. A large armadillo was flattened across the road like a pancake. Roadkill. And it was Tom's job to clean it up.

Some emergency, thought Tom as he opened the trunk of his car and took out a shovel. "This town doesn't need a sheriff," he muttered, "it needs an undertaker." As he scooped up the armadillo, Tom told the carcass, "You're going to a better place."

••••• •••••

After disposing of the armadillo, Tom felt hungry. Driving down Main Street he passed a row of boarded–up shops and abandoned cars and pulled up in front of The Office, the local bar and grill.

Nick, Larry, Jeffrey, and Evan, still damp from their shower at the school yard, were kicking around an old ball as Tom pulled up.

SLAM! Nick kicked the ball into the side of Tom's car.

"How many times do I have to tell you to keep away from the car?" chided Tom as he got out.

"How many times have you told us *today*?" teased Jeffrey.

"Hey, however many, I guess it wasn't enough, Deputy Dog," Nick added.

"Watch your mouth or I'll kick your butt," warned Tom.

"All the way to Pizza Hut?" asked Nick.

"I wish we lived in a town that *had* a Pizza Hut," said Larry wistfully.

"Move it, midgets," Tom said, pushing past the boys and heading toward The Office. "I got things to do."

"Hey!" Jeffrey called out. "You may think you know everything, but here's a news flash. Something *radical* finally happened in this town!"

"Nothing radical ever happens in this town," said Tom.

"Wrong," said Larry.

"We met our new teacher," Evan said cheerfully.

"You get a new teacher every year." Tom shrugged.

"This one's different, Deputy Dog," said Nick.

"Yeah," added Jeffrey. "*Really* different."

Tom paused. The boys had roused his interest. For these kids to get *this* excited, the new schoolteacher must really be something special. He decided he had to find out for himself. Tom got back into his patrol car and drove to Bomma Cole's farmhouse.

Bomma Cole was the schoolteacher for the elementary grades. Tom guessed that the new schoolteacher might be staying with Bomma since Elma had no hotel. When he saw an unfamiliar red convertible parked in Bomma's driveway he knew he had guessed correctly.

Bomma knew why Tom had come. "News travels fast," she said as she emerged from her house.

"It's a small town," said Tom without getting out.

"She went running," Bomma told Tom. Then she added with a laugh, "Probably looking for the easiest way out of here."

Tom thanked Bomma and drove off, a man with a

mission. It wasn't long before he saw a lone figure jogging along Old Country Road, a full two miles from Bomma's place. As he got closer he saw that the jogger was a woman in a brightly colored athletic outfit. He had found the new schoolteacher.

Tom smiled. Then he quickly combed his hair and checked it in the rearview mirror. So what if I'm not a star quarterback anymore, he thought to himself. I still got what it takes. But just in case, he decided he'd stay inside the car so the new schoolteacher wouldn't notice his slight paunch.

Tom turned on the car siren and picked up speed. He raced past the schoolteacher, noticing her head turning to see him as he whizzed by. Seconds later he slammed on the brakes and turned the car around as if on a dime. That ought to impress her, he thought. Then he gunned the engine and raced back down the road. When he came up alongside her, he slammed the brakes again and brought the car to a jolting, tire-squealing stop.

"Excuse me, ma'am," Tom said in an urgent tone, as if he were in the middle of important police business. "Sheriff Tom Palmer, Lane County. I got an APB out of Austin. Bank robbers. Heading this way. Driving a Chevy with a—" He suddenly lost his train of thought. Then he noticed the schoolteacher's jogging outfit and said, "—a white top and a red bottom. You see it?"

The schoolteacher was running in place next to the patrol car. "Only car I've seen is yours, Sheriff Tom Palmer," she replied.

"Call me Tom," he said.

"Call me Anna Montgomery, Sheriff," she said.

"You can drop the sheriff part," said Tom, blushing.

"Sorry I can't help you," Anna said, picking up her jogging again. Tom put his car into reverse and slowly followed alongside.

"Where'd you say you were from?" he asked.

"Surrey," replied Anna.

"Where?" Tom asked.

"Surrey, England," said Anna.

"I'm planning a trip to England," Tom fibbed. "Real soon. I've always been very interested in English . . . things."

"I've always been very interested in America," said Anna. "I had no idea it would look like this."

"Not a whole lot worth seeing around here," Tom said. "'Course, there are a few local points of interest. The Elma Armadillos were at one time a football powerhouse." He smiled. "That was back in the days when I played."

"Like she cares?" came a voice from behind.

Tom craned his head around. Nick, Larry, Jeffrey, and Evan had ridden up alongside his car and were brazenly eavesdropping on the conversation.

"Zip it, midgets," snapped Tom. Then he continued to Anna, "As I was saying. This town at one time had a real football dynasty. There's a billboard off Main Street, documents some of the achievements. You might want to take a look at it. That's me on the left side, 'Course, a big twister last year took off the top of my head, but you can still see the resemblance if you're coming in on Route Forty-nine."

"Aren't you worried about the bank robbers, Sheriff Tom?" Anna asked.

"Yeah, right," Tom nodded. "I got to get on that."

"You got to do something," said Jeffrey.

Tom ignored the boys. "So," he told Anna, "welcome to America." And with that Tom stepped on the gas. Only his car was still in reverse and it shot backward. Red-faced, Tom slammed the brakes and shifted into drive. The four boys howled with laughter.

"Welcome to America," Anna murmured to herself.

ANNA

"My name is Anna Montgomery. I'm from England, and I will be your teacher for the first half of your school year."

Anna had just finished writing her name on the blackboard when she turned around and introduced herself to the class. Anna then went round the room and asked the students to introduce themselves. As they said their names, Nick, Larry, Jeffrey, and Evan blushed when she smiled at them familiarly. They sat on one side of the room with the rest of the boys in the class. Across the room sat the girls.

"Hey, before you get all sweaty," Jeffrey shouted, "don't waste your time with us. We're losers."

"You're not losers," said Anna.

"Yeah, we are," said Polly. "You just don't know us very good." Her friends, Kate and Sophia, nodded.

"Didn't anybody tell you?" asked Evan. "We have the worst test scores in the state."

Anna was here to teach these kids, no matter how hopeless that might seem. And the first thing she wanted to teach them was that they were better than their test scores indicated. "So you all had a bad test day," she said breezily.

"Four years *in a row* we had bad test days," said Nick with gloomy finality.

"What's it to you, anyway?" Jeffrey asked Anna. "You just said you'd be out of here in six months."

"Six months is a long time," said Anna.

"Especially in Elma," groaned Sophia.

"We can do a lot in six months," insisted Anna. "Now, let's get to know each other," she added brightly. "Someone tell me something that makes you feel special."

There was a long silence.

"Okay," said Anna. "*I'll* start. I believe you are special because you live in America. And America is a place where you can be anything you want to be."

"I think that was before Reaganomics, ma'am," said Evan.

She tried again. "I look out at you here today, and I see ten special faces."

"That'll change once you get used to us," said Larry.

Anna sighed. There *had* to be some way to get through to these kids. "Let's think of this another way," she suggested. "What makes you different from the kid sitting next to you?"

Two hands shot up in the air. One belonged to Sue Landon. The other to her identical twin sister, Lou. "We got asthma!" Sue and Lou shouted in unison.

"Well, *that's* different," Anna said.

"*And* we've got our own inhalers," the twins added.

"That's special, too," said Anna, nodding.

"Can we use them right now?" they asked.

"Of course," said Anna.

The twins pulled two plastic inhalers out of their pockets and began breathing deeply. In and out. In and out. It was hypnotic. Soon the rest of the class was breathing deeply, too.

"Okay, come on," Anna said, interrupting. "What's so special about the rest of you guys? Evan?"

"I swallowed a pencil last year," said Evan proudly. "I could be slowly dying of lead poison. No one knows for sure."

"Right," said Anna, a tone of doubt in her voice. "We'll keep an eye on you. Tak?"

"I can burp the whole ABCs," said Tak, age eleven. "Except a *Z*. No one burps a *Z*."

"That's a skill," Anna said. "Sort of. Sophia?"

"I have a great aunt who has a beard," said Sophia. "She lives in Rome."

"I love Italy," said Anna.

"Rome, *Texas,*" corrected Sophia. "It's near Waxahachie."

"I didn't know that," admitted Anna. "Larry, what makes you special?"

"My dad has a job," Larry said proudly. Cookie was his father, owner of The Office.

"That's *very* special for this town," added Polly.

Anna looked around the room. Most of the kids had offered answers to her question.

"Kate," Anna called out cheerfully, "what makes you special?"

"My parents are divorced. Thanks for bringing it up."

A shrill bleat from outside broke the silence. It sounded like a goat.

"What's that?" asked Anna.

"First recess," answered Larry. Then the whole class filed out of the classroom.

Anna watched with dismay as her students filled the school yard and broke off into small groups. Polly sat with her goat, Ernie, which she took everywhere, including school. Sophia sat by herself leafing through a magazine. Sue and Lou braided each other's hair, and Tak fried ants with the help of a big magnifying glass. The rest of the kids just moped around.

As Anna watched her class, Bomma Cole emerged from the building followed by her class of gradeschoolers.

"How's it going, honey?" asked Bomma.

"I don't think they like school," Anna replied sadly.

Bomma tried reassuring her. "Don't take it personal. They don't like anything. Not even each other."

The Foreigners

After school Kate and Sophia waited on the steps while Polly untied Ernie from the stair railing. Their classroom window was right next to the stairs, and the girls could see the new teacher inside collecting her things.

"So what do you think?" Sophia asked Kate.

"She'll never last," Kate said.

Polly walked up with Ernie in tow, and the three girls hiked the short distance from school to Mrs. Holland's gas station. Polly's mom gave the girls a free bottle of Coke, which they passed back and forth as they sat on the stoop in front of the station.

A few minutes later a station wagon pulled up to the gas pump. It was an old, beat-up car that looked as if it either hadn't been washed in years or had been on the road for a very long time. Or maybe both. A woman and a boy were up front. Probably a mother and son. The back of the car was crowded with boxes and suitcases, and the girls figured the two of them were moving somewhere. No way could they be moving to Elma. After all, no one was *that* desperate.

The woman got out of the car and went inside the store. She handed some money to Polly's mom. Then she returned to the car. The boy climbed out and went to the gas pump and began filling the tank.

Kate watched the boy. She decided he might be Mexican, since Elma was so close to the border. He looked to be about her age, she thought. And not bad-looking, either.

After a moment the boy felt Kate's eyes on him and returned her gaze. Their eyes locked.

A battered pickup truck drove into the gas station. The truck came to a sharp stop, and a man stepped out.

Kate's face flushed red. The man was her father. And he was drunk.

"Kate, tell her to turn it on!"

Kate sighed but got up and went into the store. Sophia and Polly followed behind.

"My dad wants gas," Kate told Polly's mom.

"Sorry, Kate," said Mrs. Holland firmly. "But this isn't the United Way. I can't keep giving it away."

"Hey, it's OK," said Kate. "I understand."

"I hope your dad does," said Polly. "He sure looks like he's in a bad mood."

"Now'days he doesn't have any other mood," said Kate.

"Brenda!" they heard Mr. Mullaney shout from outside. "Get this thing going! BRENDA!"

Polly's mother went outside, followed by the girls. Kate's father was holding a gas nozzle in his hand, and Kate winced when she saw him staggering. Even by his standards he appeared drunker than normal.

"What's your problem?" he asked Polly's mother.

"My problem is you owe me too much money for any more gas to be going in that truck," said Mrs. Holland.

"I'll pay," said Kate's father. "I just don't have it right now."

"And you won't have it tomorrow. Or the next day. I got to draw the line, Ed."

"So I'm short on cash," he snapped. "Big deal. Maybe you never heard, but the factory closed!"

"And my husband hasn't worked since, either," Mrs. Holland shot back. "How dare you act like I don't know what the plant's closing means!"

"Then how come you're willing to turn against people who are hurting?"

"I got my own bills to pay," she said. "My own mouths to feed!"

Ed looked over to where the boy was pumping gas, and his face became red with anger.

"My family's lived in this town for years," he said. "But suddenly I'm nothin' and *they're* somethin'!"

The boy was about to get back in the car when Ed stepped in front of him.

"Excuse me," said the boy.

Ed shoved the boy hard, pushing him down.

"Get out of my face!" Ed shouted.

The boy's mother raced to her son, then grabbed

Kate's father by the arm, afraid he might strike her boy again.

"Dad!" Kate shouted in alarm. She ran to her father and held him back.

Tom Palmer had just driven by in his patrol car when he saw the scuffle. He turned into the gas station and got out of the car.

"We got a problem here?" asked Tom.

"No, sir," said Kate, her face hot with embarrassment and shame. "My dad was just leaving."

"Got ourselves a hot-tempered kid is all," Ed sneered as Kate guided him back to his truck.

"Excitement's over," Tom said as he watched the woman help her son up from the ground. "Let's get back to our own business."

Then Tom heard the boy and his mother speak to each other in Spanish. He had lived in this border town long enough to learn the language.

"Why did he do that?" the boy asked his mother. "I didn't do anything."

"Of course not," his mother replied. "But we're different. That's enough for some people."

Anna's Geography Lesson

Jobs were scarce in Elma, but for Larry's dad, Cookie, business was booming. The more folks didn't work, the more they hung out at The Office. And it was just about the only place in Elma that was open for business on a regular basis.

That afternoon the atmosphere in The Office was gloomy and dull. That is, normal. Cigarette and pipe smoke wafted through the air as folks sipped their beers. Some were leaning against the bar, while others sat at the few tables that were scattered about the room.

Tom Palmer had just arrived. He took his usual seat at the bar when he heard Darius shout from behind, "Show time!"

Tom turned around. Darius, who had been staring out the window, shouted from the other end of the room, "Here she comes!"

Everyone in the room leaped from their stools

and crowded around the window.

Sure enough, Anna Montgomery, the new schoolteacher, was jogging down Main Street. She was big news in Elma.

"Uh-oh," said Darius. "She's coming this way!"

They did a quick about-face and hustled back to their seats. When Anna entered the bar everyone acted as if she were just another customer.

All except Tom.

"Cookie," Tom told the bartender. "Get the young lady a beer."

"Bottled water's fine," said Anna as she approached the bar.

Cookie had never heard of bottled water, so he improvised. He took an empty beer bottle, filled it with tap water, and handed it to Anna.

"So how was your first day at school?" Tom asked Anna.

"The kids didn't have much enthusiasm," replied Anna.

"None of us do," admitted Tom.

"They explained that to me."

"You live here a while and you'll get the idea," said Tom.

"That's encouraging," said Anna as she took a drink of her water. "So how's the sheriff business?"

"This sheriff thing is strictly a temporary gig," Tom explained. "I'm very close to a big position with a multinational corporation."

"What do they do?" Anna asked.

"All kinds of things, I hope," Tom said. "I haven't settled on a corporation yet. I'm just narrowing down the list. One of them has offices in Africa. I'd go on safari on my days off."

"Sounds exciting."

Tom shrugged. "A man's got to dream," he said, blushing.

Anna sighed. "I wish I could get the kids to dream."

"If anyone could," Cookie put in kindly, "I'd put my money on you."

Anna nodded a thank-you to Cookie. Then she finished her water and put the bottle on the bar. "Well, I'm back on the road," she said and headed for the door.

Tom called after her. "Maybe we could do something together sometime?" he asked.

"Do you run?" Anna asked him.

Everyone in the room turned and looked at Tom.

"Sure, I run," Tom said. "I mean, I used to run. It's not like you forget how."

"So we'll run together," said Anna. Then she was out the door and gone.

"Yeah," Tom said half-aloud after she left. "We'll run together. Great."

••••• •••••

The following morning Anna stood in front of the classroom holding an old globe. She had just announced to the class that they would be having a lesson in geography. She was surprised that the kids had no reaction to the announcement. Not a clap. Not a groan. Nothing. They just stared blankly at her with bored expressions. It was as if even groaning was too much of an effort for them.

"Kate, will you come show the class where Columbus first landed in the New World?" Anna asked.

"You mean get up?" asked Kate.

"Yes."

"I don't get up," said Kate. "For anybody."

Just then the classroom door opened and Bomma entered, her hands around the shoulders of a young boy. Kate, Sophia, and Polly recognized the boy immediately as the one Kate's dad shoved at the gas station the day before.

"Class," announced Bomma, "I'd like you to meet Juan Morales. He's new in town, and he's joining your class."

Bomma handed Juan over to Anna. Juan quickly took a seat in the back of the classroom. Then she asked the class to make their new classmate feel at home.

"Pull up a cot and get a pillow," Larry whispered to Juan. "We're in the middle of geology."

"*Geography*," Anna corrected.

"Whatever," Larry said with a shrug.

Anna sighed. No matter how hard she tried, nothing seemed to work. It was more than frustrating. It was sad. These kids had given up on life before they'd even had a chance to live it.

She tried again. "Let's everyone please focus their attention," she said. "Juan, we are studying world geography."

"*She's* studying world geography," Nick leaned over and whispered into Jeffrey's ear. "*We're* bored out of our minds."

For Anna, that was the last straw. She angrily snapped the globe out of its holder and held it up in front of the class.

"Will someone tell me what's wrong with this globe?"

"You just broke it?" asked Polly.

"No. It's outdated. Times have changed. Many countries in the world are no longer the same."

"Texas is still Texas," said Jeffrey.

"There's more to this world than Texas," said Anna.

Kate said, "Not from where I sit." This made Sophia and Polly giggle.

Anna let the globe drop, but before it hit the floor she flipped it back up with her foot. Then she bounced it from her left knee to her right knee, then back again. Next, she sent the globe up into the air, bounced it twice off her forehead, then let it fall to her foot, kicked it up and back over her shoulder and then kicked it straight back. The globe slammed against the blackboard and then ricocheted into a wastepaper basket that stood next to Anna's desk.

The kids watched all this in stunned silence.

"Where did you learn to do *that*?" asked Larry.

"Prison," joked Anna.

"*What?!*" the kids muttered in shocked disbelief.

"That was a joke," she explained. "I learned how to do that at school in England. Which is another country, far from Texas."

Anna smiled to herself. At last! They had

suddenly come to life. Now all she had to do was turn that spark of interest into a fire.

Anna led them out of the classroom to the school gymnasium. She glanced around the old gymnasium and then walked over to a closet door marked EQUIPMENT.

"We're gonna learn something together," Anna told the kids. "Something everyone can participate in!"

"There's nothing in there except dead mice, ma'am," Polly said.

"Then we'll learn about mice," Anna said with determination. She yanked open the closet door. To everyone's surprise the closet wasn't filled with mice, just a few moths. Anna waved away the moths and dug into the closet. A few seconds later she pulled out an old, scuffed, kick ball.

"Here we have it," Anna said, holding the ball up for them to see. "A football."

The kids looked at Anna.

"I don't think so," said Nick.

"It's Mrs. Curdley's old kick ball," said Larry.

"No," said Anna. "It's a ball. And if we use it for football, it becomes a football."

"Ma'am," interjected Evan. "Football's aren't round. They look more like lemons."

Anna understood why the kids were so confused. "What I call football, you call soccer," she explained. "This is a soccer ball!"

"Are you feeling okay, ma'am?" asked Polly. "It's all right with us if you want to chew garlic pills."

"I'm feeling better than I have in days," Anna said,

smiling. "We are going to learn soccer."

Sue and Lou said, "We don't play soccer."

"Yeah," Nick said. "It's for foreigners."

"Well, I'm a foreigner," Anna reminded Nick.

"Well, we're *American,"* said Sue and Lou.

"And we don't like soccer," added Tak.

Anna frowned. "You guys don't like anything," she said. "The boys don't like the girls. Kate doesn't talk to anyone. Polly talks to a goat. The twins talk only to themselves. And nobody speaks to Tak. Juan's going to fit right in. Well, all that's going to change, whether you like it or not." Anna pointed to the door. "Outside, everybody. Today's lesson has changed. You're going to learn how to play soccer!"

Signs of Life

Anna led the kids out to the school yard.

"In soccer you don't use your hands," she said dropping the ball to her feet.

"We know that," grunted Nick.

Anna continued. "But just because you can't use your hands, doesn't mean you can't use your body."

The school bell rang. "Whoever would like to try should stay after school," Anna told the kids. "We'll have a practice."

The kids exchanged looks. They decided to stay.

Only the new kid, Juan Morales, walked away.

"Juan, where are you going?" asked Anna. "We need you. Don't you want to try?"

Juan didn't answer. He didn't even turn around. He just walked out of the school yard and down the road, until he was out of sight.

"Okay, he's new," Anna explained to the rest of the boys and girls. "He's shy. He'll come on board later."

Then she rolled the ball to Nick. "Give it a kick," she told him.

Nick gave it a powerful spike, just as if he were kicking a can into the middle of the road. The ball shot high into the air and disappeared into the street. Anna smiled, impressed. There may be signs of life in Elma, after all, she thought optimistically.

All the kids ran into the middle of the street in search of the ball. Suddenly, they were distracted by the wailing of a police siren.

"Hold it right there, youngsters," came the voice of Sheriff Tom Palmer over his patrol car loudspeaker. The kids stopped when they saw his car rolling slowly up the road.

"Good thing I happened to be in the area, ma'am," Tom said to Anna as he pulled to a stop. "You know, cars come whizzing down this street like there's no tomorrow."

Anna threw Tom a suspicious look. "I haven't seen a car pass all day except yours, Sheriff Tom," she told him. "Five times."

"Just doing my job, ma'am," said Tom with a blush. The kids giggled.

"*Ooooh,*" Nick said in a singsong voice. "Deputy Dog's in *lo-ove*. Deputy Dog's in *love.*"

Then the rest of the kids joined in, "*Deputy Dog's in love, Deputy Dog's in love,*" they chanted.

Tom saw one of the kids holding the soccer ball. He climbed out of his car. "So what's going on?" he asked Anna.

"We're playing football," Anna told him.

"This isn't football," said Tom. "I know football."

"This is what the rest of the world calls football, Sheriff Tom," Anna insisted. Then she turned to the kids and said, "OK, get into a circle and kick the ball back and forth to each other. This is called passing."

"Passing is in the air," Tom told Anna as the kids formed a circle and began kicking the ball around. "It's with a pigskin. It's 'First and ten, do it again.'"

Anna caught sight of some rusty metal drums sitting by the school shed. "Give me a hand," she said to Tom, "and we'll discuss it."

Tom helped Anna roll four of the drums into the school yard. Then they set two up at either end of the field, forming two makeshift goalposts. The kids played carelessly and with abandon, and only occasionally stopped long enough to take pointers from Tom and Anna. But that was fine with Anna. Everybody was having fun—except for Kate, who stood on the sidelines scowling.

"OK, that's it for today!" Anna finally shouted through Tom's police megaphone. The kids had been playing for nearly an hour, and it was starting to get dark.

Much to Anna's surprise, the kids groaned. They didn't want to stop! Even Kate, who *had* spent most of the time watching, was disappointed.

"Good! Great!" exclaimed Anna as the kids fell to the ground, exhausted. "What a start! You showed so much potential!"

"You were awful," Tom whispered to the boys, so Anna couldn't hear.

"Now listen, everyone," Anna continued. "While you were practicing I called the school board and joined a league. Our first game is tomorrow in Austin."

The kids stared at Anna, stunned. They hadn't expected this.

"Tomorrow?" asked Larry. "You mean like the day after today?"

"That's what we call tomorrow," said Tom.

"In Austin?" asked Sue and Lou.

"That's like a million miles away," said Nick. "Forget it."

"All you have to do is believe in yourself," insisted Anna.

"Why?" asked Tak.

"Just try," said Anna. "Sheriff Tom and I believe in you. Don't we, Sheriff Tom?"

"Uh—oh—yeah," Tom lied. "Sure."

"Even if we did decide to go," began Kate. "How are we going to get there? Walk?"

Anna turned to Tom. "Sheriff Tom, could you do me a personal favor?"

"Name it," said Tom eagerly.

"Help me drive the kids to Austin."

"Hey," said Tom, "I'd love to." It was pretty obvious, however, that he could think of at least a hundred things he'd really rather do.

"One more request," Anna added after doing a quick head count of the kids. There were ten all together.

"Anything."

"I'm short a player. What do you think?"

"I'd never pass for a twelve-year-old," Tom replied jokingly.

"I meant, what about finding us another kid?"

explained Anna.

"What d'you say, Deputy Dog?" shouted Larry. "You going to help us?"

Tom frowned, thinking. Then he pulled Anna aside.

"Look," he told her. "I'll drive the midgets to Austin. I'll get another player. I'll paint the stadium if you want. But you've got to do one thing for me."

"What?" asked Anna.

"Get them to stop calling me Deputy Dog!"

The Big City

That evening, ten-year-old Newt was ambling along the road near Miller's Creek collecting junk in his wagon. It was what he always did this time of day. When he was done collecting, he would take the wagonload of junk home and catalog each and every item in his mind. It was his favorite thing to do.

Newt suddenly felt as if he were being watched. He turned around and noticed that Sheriff Palmer was driving slowly behind him.

"Hey, Newt!" Tom said, pulling up beside the boy. "What's up?"

"Not much," replied Newt. "I got part of a tailpipe and an old shoe. You seen anything good?"

"Nah," said Tom. "Look, I came to ask you to play soccer with the big kids. They're starting a team, and we're down a player."

Newt's face lit up. Nobody had ever asked him to play with the big kids before. He agreed on the spot.

"Good," said Tom. "We got a game tomorrow."

"Wow! A game!" said Newt. Then he tilted his neck and scratched his head and asked, "What's soccer anyway?"

Tom rolled his eyes. "It's sort of like kick ball mixed with hockey," he explained.

"Hey," said Newt with a smile. "I don't know much about kick ball *or* hockey—but I'm your man!"

••••• •••••

Tom met Anna in front of the schoolhouse the next morning. Nick, Jeffrey, Larry, Evan, Tak, and Newt piled into Tom's patrol car. Kate, Sophia, Polly, and the twins rode in Anna's convertible. Even Ernie the goat came along for the ride.

The only one who didn't come along was Juan. He walked home alone but watched the kids drive off. Kate saw him and turned around in her seat to watch him.

A little more than an hour later, they reached Austin. They drove past what looked like a model community. All the houses were identical, with expensive cars in the driveways.

They reached the Austin High stadium just before noon. An enormous playing field stretched before them as they pulled up behind the school. The field was immaculate. The grass was freshly mowed, and the boundary lines had been freshly painted. Across one end of the field a black-and-silver banner rippled in the wind. An elaborate insignia, two swords crossed over a soccer ball, was embroidered into the banner, followed by the words *Austin Knights.* Alongside the banner stood a full-size suit of armor.

Its freshly polished metal gleamed and sparkled in the sunlight.

A group of eleven boys, all dressed in matching black rugby tops and silver shorts, was practicing on the field as the Elma kids piled out of the cars. The home team moved across the soccer field like a well-drilled battalion of battle-tested marines. These kids were amazing. These kids were awesome. These kids were the Austin Knights.

When the kids from Elma saw who they were up against, they felt sick. They didn't have uniforms. They didn't have banners. They didn't have a full-size suit of armor, either. Worse, they didn't have a clue how to play soccer. All they had were their torn jeans, worn-out sneakers, and a lazy old goat.

When one of the Knights caught sight of the Elma kids, he let out with a loud guffaw. "*That's* the team we're playing?" he asked, laughing.

"They don't look like a team," laughed another Knight.

"What're they called?" asked another.

"The hicks from the sticks," yet another sneered.

"Hey!" the first Knight called out to the Elma kids. "What do you turkeys call yourselves?"

The kids looked at one another questioningly.

"What's our name?" Polly asked Jeffrey.

"We don't have a name," replied Jeffrey with a shrug.

Larry shouted at the Knights, "We'll tell you later!"

Suddenly Ernie the goat stepped out from Anna's car with a grunt. The Knights exploded with laughter.

"Hey, they brought a goat!" a Knight shouted.

Kate scowled at the boy. "He just *happened* to be in the car," she told him. "We didn't bring him on purpose."

Meanwhile, Tom and Anna had gone off in search of the Knights' coach. They found him standing near one of the corner arcs, dressed in the same silver and black as the boys on the field. He was talking into a mobile phone. When Anna and Tom approached him, the man looked up. He nearly froze when he saw Tom.

"Oh, no," Tom muttered to Anna. "I know him."

"He looks tough," said Anna.

"He was always a pinhead," Tom said.

Tom and the Knights coach shook hands, but Anna could tell that there was no love lost between the two men.

"Tom," said the man. "Long time no see."

"It's been a few years," the Sheriff replied.

When the Knights coach saw Anna, he looked her up and down. "Well, *va-va-voom*," he crooned. "I'm Jay Huffer. Tom and I played football together. That was back in the days when we were both young."

"Was that back when you were a pinhead?" Anna asked him innocently.

Tom's face turned red. "She's from England," he explained. "There's a language barrier. Jay, this is Anna Montgomery. She's an exchange teacher in Elma."

"I can't imagine coming all the way from England to that one-horse town," Jay said.

"They have more than one horse now," said Anna.

"Spare me," he said. "I got out the day I graduated." Then he looked straight at Tom and added, "Only losers stick around."

Tom had to fight to restrain himself. "I'm leaving soon myself," he lied. "I got several different possibilities."

"Oh, I bet," said Jay in a mocking tone. "You still got that shovel in your trunk?"

"Got two," replied Tom. "One's a deluxe model. It's for the big stuff. Bought it mail order."

"My son's the lead scorer," Huffer said as he pointed to one of the boys on the field. "How's your kid do?"

"I don't have a kid," said Tom.

"Really? And you're coaching? Why bother?"

"Love of the game," Tom said.

Huffer shook his head sympathetically as he glanced at the ragtag group of kids from Elma. "What's the story on your team?" he asked Tom. "They sure look young. My goodness, you've got *girls* out here. In our league the girls have their own teams."

"We don't have enough kids for that," said Tom.

"So you're playing with a bunch of little kids and *girls*?"

"Yes," Anna interjected.

Huffer laughed. "I guess you haven't heard. "We *won* the league championship last year. We were *undefeated*!"

"Might be different this year," Tom said.

DAY OF THE KNIGHTS

The game was about to begin, and Jeffrey found himself looking down at a soccer ball that the Austin referee had just rolled to his feet. He looked up, puzzled. The referee had to explain to Jeffrey that he was supposed to start the game with a kick-off from the center spot on the field. No sweat, Jeffrey thought.

The Knights were assembled downfield in three neat rows. They looked eager and ready to pounce. The Elma kids, on the other hand, were loosely scattered on the field in no particular order or formation. In fact, a few looked as if they'd rather be someplace else. Even Elma.

Anna had briefly explained the rules of the game to the kids before they left Elma. There were two goal nets, each on opposite ends of the field. Players had to maneuver the ball into the opponents' net to score a point. But they had to do this without using their hands. The only players allowed to use their hands were the goalies.

Anna had assigned positions: Jeffrey, Nick, and Sophia were forwards. Sue, Lou, and Newt were midfielders. Kate, Polly, Evan, and Tak took up the rear defense. Larry, because he couldn't run and couldn't kick, was assigned to the goal net.

Anna had run them through some basic practice drills, too. First they learned the offensive moves: dribbles, chip passes, back passes. Then the defensive ones: marking and tackling. Finally, Anna showed the kids how to shoot and volley the ball.

Unfortunately, by game time the Elma kids had forgotten most everything Anna had taught them. The kids wandered around the field aimlessly. They couldn't remember their positions on the field.

BLEEEE! The ref blew his whistle, and almost immediately Anna groaned. Jeffrey, instead of passing to a teammate, had kicked the ball straight to a Knight!

The surprised Knight player lofted the ball into the air with his foot and passed it to the striker. Then a left midfielder went running past the center spot into Elma territory. The striker pushed the ball to the running midfielder, who quickly gained control of it. He dribbled in and around the Elma defenders with ease as he raced for their goal.

Larry grew terrified as he watched the midfielder running toward him. His imagination took over. As if by magic, the Knight midfielder was transformed into a *real* knight, complete with chain mail armor. And he was galloping toward him on a huge horse!

Larry panicked and covered his eyes with his hands. Then he felt a gust of wind whip by his head. When he opened his eyes the knight was a midfielder again. He had just kicked the ball past Larry's head and scored the first point for Austin.

The Austin Knights cheered.

Forty-five minutes later the Knights were still cheering. The first half of the game was over, and they were ahead 10–0.

Jay Huffer gathered his team around him. "Men," he said in a voice loud enough so that the Elma kids could hear, "we're ten to zip. What do we do when we are clearly superior to the enemy?"

"Go for the throat!" answered a Knight.

Huffer looked at the boy and smiled. It was his son, Jay Junior.

"Exactly," the coach replied, proudly tousling his son's hair. "We do *not* back off! We go for the kill! Make them pay for even *thinking* of playing against the Knights!"

From the other side of the field, Tom watched Huffer exhort his team. He remembered his own playing days as a star quarterback on a championship team. Winning had felt so good. Then he turned to face the Elma kids, who were huddled around Anna, and sighed. These kids looked as if they had just gone ten rounds with George Foreman, he thought.

"This is a learning experience," Anna reassured them.

"Why?" asked Jeffrey. "We already know how to fall down."

"My feet hurt," complained Polly.

Tak said, "My shins hurt. They keep kicking me."

Everyone was in the dumps except Newt. He was smiling!

"Newt, are you okay?" Anna asked him. She worried that he might have been kicked in the head.

"I just can't believe you asked me to play," Newt said. "Nobody ever asks me to do anything."

"You're all doing great," Tom told the kids. "Sort of. Kate, you could go after the ball more."

"I've been watching them eat turf for the last half hour," Kate scowled. "I'm not doing that."

"Let's just get back in there and have a good time," Anna said as the half was about to begin.

"Hey," complained Jeffrey. "We may not be the sharpest tools in the shed, but we know the difference between a good time and a bad time!"

Then Larry added, "And *this* is definitely *not* a good time."

••••• •••••

Things only got worse for Elma in the second half. The Knights, merciless in their play, scored point after point after point.

It was a comedy of errors, and the Elma kids were the big stars.

On one play, Nick tried to block a Knight striker as he crossed the center spot, but as Nick tried to steal the ball he went sliding across the grass and missed.

On another play, a Knight right winger dribbled in and around Elma's loose defense. Evan, on the defense line, tried to act as a stopper and mark the player. But the Knight countered. In one move he flicked the ball up and head-butted it at Evan. The ball smacked Evan in the forehead and knocked him backward onto the ground. The Knight then casually retrieved the ball and smashed it into the goal net for yet another point.

Newt, playing midfield, had tried to stop a Knight who was dribbling toward him. The Knight didn't even bother to sidestep Newt. Instead, he bore down on Newt like a sixteen-wheeler diesel truck and—*Oomph*!—Newt went flying.

"Cool!" Newt shouted when he landed on his back. "Playing with the big boys!"

Kate had not been so anxious to have her limbs rearranged. In fact, she had spent most of the game avoiding any contact with the Knights. Positioned in the backfield, she lingered as close to the sidelines as possible. On one play, however, a Knight had dribbled downfield, right toward her.

"Kate, get in there!" shouted Anna. "Tackle him!"

"Tackle him?" Tom asked Anna. "This isn't football."

"Tackle means to get the ball away from him," explained Anna.

"Does Kate know that?" Tom asked.

"Tackle him," Kate repeated to herself as she watched the Knight dribble toward her.

Just as the Knight dribbled by, she stuck out her leg. The Knight tripped and went sprawling facedown into the dirt. Kate smiled. Maybe I could get into this after all, she thought.

But on the sidelines Anna groaned.

"Penalty kick!" shouted Jay Huffer.

The referee blew his whistle and signaled a foul. Then he placed the ball for the penalty shot.

The Elma kids lined up in front of their goal, and Jay Junior came up to the ball. Jay Junior had a crazy, mad-scientist grin on his face. One by one they stepped out of his line of fire. Tom and Anna signaled for them to get back in formation, but none of them moved.

Jay Junior's kick blew into the net like a shot from a cannon. Then, finally, the ref blew the whistle and the game ended. The Knights had won, 18–0.

The Knights cheered in victory. *"Two-four-six-eight,"* they chanted, *"who did we decimate?"*

"What were their names again?" Jay Junior asked.

"The Losers?" asked one Knight.

"The Hicks?" asked another.

"The Goats?" asked yet another, laughing.

"They're not even good enough to have a name!" said Jay Junior.

"They're the Nothings from nowhere!" a teammate suggested.

The Knights resumed the chant.

> "*Two-four-six-eight,*
> *Who did we decimate?*
> *The Nothings! The Nothings!*
> *YAAAAAAYYYYY!!!*"

"We're *not* the Nothings!" Sophia shouted angrily across the field at the Knights. "We're the *Elma* Nothings!"

"Will you shut up?" Nick told Sophia.

Jay Huffer ambled up to Tom and Anna with a cocky grin on his face.

"We're a high-scoring team," he said. "But eighteen to nil? That's big, even for us." Jay was enjoying humiliating the Elma team. "A suggestion? Lose the girls. On second thought, lose them all. These kids aren't cut out for the game. Find some players with talent." He turned to walk away, then paused. "'Course, I have no idea how you're going to do that in Elma. *Victory lap, men!*"

Huffer jogged back to his team and joined them in a lap around the field.

"What a total jerk," muttered Kate.

"Hey, you tried," Tom told the kids.

"And we're proud of you," added Anna.

"Why?" asked Jeffrey. "We stank."

"Well, technically speaking, yes," Tom nodded.

"But you played," added Anna. "That's what's important."

"What's important is that we never play again," said Larry.

The kids all nodded in agreement and began heading back to the cars. And back to Elma.

"They'll probably feel different about this after a good night's sleep," Anna told Tom.

"I wouldn't count on it," said Tom.

Go Climb A Mountain

The next day, Anna and Tom were standing in front of the Elma schoolhouse waiting for the kids to show up for practice. They were half an hour late, and there was still no sign of them.

"You can hardly blame them," said Tom. "It could take years to get over a defeat like that."

Anna angrily kicked a soccer ball against the door of Tom's patrol car. "I don't get this town!" she exclaimed. "You're all a bunch of quitters!"

"Would a quitter be standing here on a Saturday?" replied Tom. "Anyway," he joked, "soccer is my life."

"Please . . . ," Anna groaned.

"I didn't have any life before so it was an easy transition," he quipped.

But Anna wasn't ready to give up on these kids. "You know," she told Tom. "I had a coach who used to tell us that you'd never get to the top of the mountain by standing in a field."

"I guess the guy wasn't a rocket scientist," said Tom.

"He was amazing," said Anna. "And the metaphor works. We were all in a field, and he made us find the mountain. That's what I want to do here with these kids."

Tom looked at Anna for a long moment. It had been a long time since anyone in Elma had cared much about anything. Maybe, he thought, she was beginning to rub off on him. The fact was, Tom was beginning to care, too.

"Hey, I'm with you, I swear," he told Anna. "Give me the afternoon, and I'll see if I can sign anyone else up for the hike."

••••• •••••

A few minutes later Tom found Sophia and Polly standing in the middle of a road planting crushable objects in the path of oncoming cars. Tom turned on his emergency lights and pulled over to the side of the road.

"How many times have I told you to keep this junk out of the road?" he asked.

"However many, it wasn't enough," answered Sophia.

"This time we're going to your parents," he threatened. "Unless, of course, you are willing to climb a mountain."

Sophia and Polly threw each other a quizzical look. "What the—"

••••• •••••

"There's no mountain around here," said Tak as he peered through his binoculars. Tom had found Tak birdwatching high up in the branches of a tree.

"It's a saying, Tak," Tom shouted from the ground. "C'mon. You're smart enough to figure it out."

Tak looked over and saw Sophia and Polly in the backseat of Tom's patrol car. No way, he thought, shaking his head.

"We got creamed," Tak said. "What's the point?"

All of a sudden, Tak grabbed hold of a branch as the tree began to rattle. Tom was trying to shake him down!

"Okay, forget the mountain," Tom said, losing his patience. "The point is, I haven't had a date in months and *you're* not going to mess it up for me!"

Tak lost his footing and plummeted to the ground.

"Sorry, Tak," he said as he helped the boy to his feet. "You okay? How's the old kicking foot?"

Tak looked Tom straight in the face. "Is *this* your idea of being a coach?" he asked.

••••• •••••

Sue and Lou were in their barn sitting on matching ponies and wearing matching overalls when Tom found them and asked them to come climb the mountain.

"WE WANT UNIFORMS!" the twins demanded together.

"Okay," agreed Tom. "We'll get uniforms."

"They'll have to match," said Lou.

"If you wear uniforms, everyone will match," Tom assured them. "You're on a team, remember?"

Lou pointed to her sister and said, "We *are* a team. Remember?"

“Of course,” agreed Tom.

“And we’ll want the same number,” added Sue.

Tom furrowed his brow in exasperation. “You *can’t* wear the *same* uniform and the *same* number! People won’t be able to tell you apart!”

Sue and Lou burst out with big smiles. “Exactly!” they said.

Then they followed Tom outside to his car and piled in alongside Tak, Polly, and Sophia.

••••• •••••

Tom found Kate sitting staring between the planks of the boarded-up window of the old dress shop. A mannequin was still in the storefront wearing the same pretty pink evening gown it had been dressed in two years earlier when the store had gone out of business.

Kate was startled when Tom walked up behind her. His car was parked in the street, and inside it she could see the other kids he had rounded up. She knew instantly what he wanted and turned him down flat.

Then Tom pulled a pair of handcuffs from his belt and stepped toward Kate.

“Deal?” he asked, holding out the cuffs.

Kate looked at the handcuffs for a minute. She had always wanted them for her own.

“I didn’t say I’d play,” Kate said as she took the handcuffs from Tom. “But I’ll stand on the field and watch.”

Tom just rolled his eyes.

••••• •••••

Tom dropped the kids off with Anna at the school

yard. Then he drove around until he found Nick, Larry, Jeffrey, and Evan counting along with the second hand of the old clock in the town square.

The boys didn't want to play another soccer game. And they didn't care a hoot about mountain climbing.

"Well, what would it take to get you to go to practice?" Tom asked. By this time he was prepared to do anything.

The boys eyed Tom's car. Tom knew exactly what they wanted.

"I don't know about this," said Tom. "The mountain thing worked for everyone else."

"Yeah, well, they're stupid," said Larry.

Tom paused and thought for a moment. "Okay," he agreed. "One lesson a piece. Five minutes. No telling anyone. Ever."

Minutes later each boy was taking a turn behind the wheel.

When the driving lessons were done, Tom and the boys headed back toward the school. On the way they saw Newt, who was walking along the road pulling his red wagon full of newfound junk.

"Hey, sure I'll play!" Newt said eagerly when Tom asked him to climb the mountain. "Nobody ever asks me to do anything! And I never even knew we had mountains around here!"

By midday all the kids had been assembled at the school yard. That's when Anna realized that someone was missing.

Tom had one more stop to make.

JUAN

The trailer park was situated about a mile from the Elma town limits. It was a desolate area filled with several homes on wheels. Tom knew that most of the families that lived there were Mexican immigrants who had come to Elma a few years back. That was when the mill was open and Elma still had a future. Things had changed rather quickly in recent times. Many of the new immigrants moved on to new towns, but some still stayed, hoping, like Tom did, that Elma would one day prosper again.

The trailer park was the most likely place Juan Morales and his mother might be, Tom deduced after Anna asked him to find Juan and convince him to join the soccer team. Anna wanted desperately for Juan to become part of the class.

Some men were kicking around a soccer ball when Tom drove into the trailer park. It was the way they spent most of their time these days. Tom knew the men and asked them if they had seen a woman and a boy who were new to the park. The men pointed to a trailer at the far end of the park, and Tom drove over to it. Then he went to the front door and knocked.

Juan's mother, the woman Tom had seen in the scuffle with Ed at the gas station a few days earlier, opened the door.

"Mrs. Morales?" asked Tom.

Her face turned cold when she saw Tom's uniform and patrol car.

"What do you want?" Mrs. Morales asked Tom cautiously. "My kid didn't do anything."

"Of course not," said Tom. He smiled, trying to make Mrs. Morales feel at ease. "I'm here as a coach. Miss Montgomery's trying to get a soccer team going over at the school."

"Juan doesn't play soccer," said Mrs. Morales flatly.

"None of the kids do," replied Tom.

"He doesn't like sports," added Mrs. Morales.

"Maybe he'll learn to," said Tom. "It's an after-school thing."

"I want him to come home right after school," insisted Mrs. Morales. Then she started to close the door.

"Look," Tom said, stopping the door gently with his hand. "I'm sorry about the trouble the other day. You wanna think about it—?"

"No."

Mrs. Morales closed the door.

Tom turned to leave, but he saw Juan's face in a window.

After Tom left, Juan asked his mother, “Why?”

“I explained why,” Mrs. Morales answered.

“But if I don’t play soccer, I’ll never make any friends,” said Juan.

“I’m your friend,” said Mrs. Morales.

“You’re my *mother*,” Juan shot back unhappily.

“There’s no reason to make friends,” said Mrs. Morales. “We’ll only be here for a very short time. You’ll just be sadder when we leave.”

Angry, Juan stormed out of the room.

THE GRANARY

The kids stood in the school yard and waited as Tom and Anna approached them with soccer balls.

"OK," began Tom. "You guys experienced the agony of defeat. Big time. I first started playing organized sports when I was your age. Right over there on the Big Green. And we weren't very good at first, but we never gave up."

"Hey, I got a question," Larry blurted out.

"Good," said Tom. "Participation is the right way to start. Fire away, big guy."

"While you're here," Larry began, "who's giving speeding tickets and scraping dead animals off the highway?"

The other kids burst out laughing.

"OK," Tom said. "First rule: no questions. About anything."

"Come on," said Kate with a groan. "You don't fool us. You don't know jack about soccer."

Ten hostile faces were looking at Tom. He said, "I may not know all the rules, but I know a thing or two about kicking the ball. Check this out, Miss Attitude."

Tom took the soccer ball and drop-kicked it. The ball soared high into the air, across the field. The kids' mouths dropped open in admiration.

"Now I can see why they put you on the billboard," Sophia told Tom.

"If you practice," said Anna as she stepped closer to the kids, "maybe someday the town will make a billboard for *you* guys."

Newt thought about what Anna said for a second. "What d'ya think they'd do with the stuff on the old billboard?" he asked, slightly confused. "There's some money to be paid there."

"Before we could ever have a billboard, we'd hafta have a name," said Evan.

"Yeah," said Jeffrey. "Even bad teams have names."

"How about the Big Green?" suggested Newt. "You know, like the old sign. It's our field."

The rest of the kids liked the idea. They nodded in agreement. Newt was surprised.

"So we're the Big Green," said Jeffrey proudly.

"No one plays well without practice," Anna told the kids. "We start with the basics. Soccer training involves four areas. Fitness. Technique. Tactics. And game psychology."

"I knew that," muttered Tom.

"Form two lines," Anna told everybody.

The kids began splitting into two groups. Girls in one line. Boys in another.

Anna told Tom, "Coach Tom, you may as well get in line with them. You look like you've had one too many nacho plates."

"Ma'am," interjected Larry. "If I ran for an hour it would kill me."

"Me, too," said Tom as he fell into the boys' line.

"That's right," said Anna. "So we work up to the hour. Today we run for twelve minutes! Let's go!" And Anna took off across the field. The kids remained in their spots and watched as their teacher receded into the distance.

"Hey, you heard her, midgets!" shouted Tom. "Get your butts in gear! Go!"

The kids groaned collectively. But they began to run.

When the twelve-minute jog was over, Anna gathered the kids back onto the recess field. For the rest of that afternoon she taught them everything about soccer. She showed them frontal block tackles, cross field passes, and how to blindside the opponent.

When practice was over, the kids were dirty, sweaty, and tired.

But they felt great.

••••• •••••

"So what do you think?" asked Sophia. Practice was over and she, Polly, and Kate were heading home.

"We'll never last!" Kate said jokingly, and the three girls broke into laughter.

Turning a corner and heading along Main Street, the girls passed The Office. Kate glanced through the window. Her smile was replaced with her usual scowl. Hunched over one of the bar stools was a familiar sight: her father, Ed.

"See you guys," Kate said to Sophia and Polly as she crossed the street.

"You wanna come to my house?" Polly offered.

Kate shook her head. Then she turned around and started running.

Kate ran for several blocks. She had started out in no particular direction, but when she stopped she found herself standing in front of the old granary building.

Kate walked around to the back. She climbed an old rusted ladder that led to a small window high at the top of the building. The window was still open from the last time she had climbed through it.

Inside was a small room. Several pictures were tacked to the wall. Her Walkman and tapes were on a milk crate. And there was a coffee can filled with candy, too. It was Kate's secret hiding place.

Kate relaxed as she popped a tape into her Walkman.

But just as she was about to slip the headphones over her ears she heard a thumping noise from below. Like someone was bouncing a ball . . .

She put down her Walkman and leaned forward. Her room was actually a loft that looked down over the main space of the granary warehouse. She peered over the edge of the catwalk and saw that someone was kicking a soccer ball against the walls.

It was Juan Morales, the new kid at school.

Kate leaned over to get a better look and knocked

the coffee can filled with candy over the edge of the catwalk. Juan spun around, startled.

"Hey!" he shouted. "Who's there?" But he couldn't see anybody at first.

"What are you doing here?" Kate shouted from above.

Juan looked up and saw Kate. "You first," he said.

"I've been coming here for years," said Kate. "This is my place."

"OK," said Juan. "I'll leave."

Kate watched as Juan headed for the door. "Wait," she called out. "I'm coming down." Kate climbed down the ladder. "So you can play soccer," she commented when she was face-to-face with Juan.

Juan held the soccer ball between his arm and waist. "Yup," he replied.

"If Anna or Tom saw how good you are, they'd positively drool," said Kate. "How come it's a secret?"

Juan said simply, "I got my reasons."

Kate shrugged. "OK," she said. "Stay and kick the ball. I'm finished in here anyway. Besides, soon I won't need this place. I'll just run away for real."

"Running away is no good," said Juan.

"How would you know?"

"Just be happy you can say you were born in the U.S.A." was Juan's answer.

"Yeah," Kate agreed. "Too bad it had to be the Elma part of it."

And with that, Kate headed out the door.

The Answer

The next morning, Anna walked up and down the aisles of her classroom. The kids sat hunched over their desks trying to do the math worksheets Anna had passed out. When she reached Kate's desk, she noticed that Kate's worksheet was empty and she was drawing doodles in the margins.

"Kate," she whispered. "I *know* you can do this."

"Come on," Kate answered back. "I'm probably going to end up at a supermarket, so what difference does it make?"

"I know how smart you are," insisted Anna. "And checkers at supermarkets need math, too."

"No they don't," said Kate. "They got all those little black stripes on all the things. It adds stuff automatic."

"Giving up before you've ever really started is a sad way to live your life," said Anna. "If you keep your talents hidden or undiscovered, you only cheat yourself."

Kate looked up and saw that Juan was staring at her. He was smiling, obviously finding her trouble amusing.

"Why don't you all worry about your own work!" she snapped. Now the whole class was looking at Kate.

"Kate's right," Anna said to Juan. "Everyone get back to work."

That afternoon during recess, the kids broke into two teams to start up their soccer practice. Kate immediately scooped up the ball and threw it angrily at Juan, who was walking away. "Maybe Juan's got some hidden talents," Kate said.

"No way," said Jeffrey. "He doesn't play."

"Juan doesn't look very athletic," said Larry.

"Like *you do*?" Sophia shouted out.

Juan's face hardened. He was insulted by Larry's comment.

"You gonna play goalie?" he shouted at Larry.

"I always play goalie," Larry shouted back.

"Mind if I take a few shots against you?" asked Juan.

"*You* gonna play?" Jeffrey asked in astonishment.

"Don't worry," replied Juan. His eyes were firmly planted on Larry. "I'm not very athletic." He flipped the ball up with his feet in one smooth move. Then he said, "Get in the net, Larry."

Now everyone was staring at Larry.

"Hey, what did I do?" asked Larry as he trudged between the two metal drums that stood in for goal-posts.

Juan waited until Larry was standing in the goal

Sheriff Tom Palmer stops to meet the new schoolteacher, Anna.

The boys have nothing better to do but wait for the pigeons to begin their feeding frenzy.

Anna tries to get her class's attention.

She takes the class outside to their recreation field: The Big Green.

Anna thinks soccer might be interesting for them.

Anna was right—the team practices indoors . . .

and out—in sunshine . . .

and in the rain!

Anna and Tom can't get them to stop even when it's pouring.

Jay Huffer, the coach of the Knights, wants to intimidate the Big Green—and he does!

Larry can't help imagining knights coming at him while he's the goalie.

The Big Green finally wins against the Knights because of Newt's shot on goal!

The Big Green gets Jay Huffer's goat as he kisses Ernie—right on the smacker!

The team and the rest of the town of Elma celebrate their championship.

area. Then he dropped the soccer ball and began dribbling it across the field. Juan's moves were precise and controlled. He seemed to know where the soccer ball was going before it got there. It was obvious to everybody that Juan had been playing for a very long time.

"We don't look like that when we've got the ball," said Polly as she watched from the sidelines with the others.

"You think he's done this before?" asked Tak.

To Nick the answer was obvious. "I think he's done this *a lot* before," he said.

Juan directed the ball closer to the goal area swiftly and efficiently. He trapped it several times, alternating between both feet, using both the outsides *and* the insides of his feet as he went. When he was close enough to the goal area, he moved to the right and pulled his leg back, readying the kick. Seeing the kick coming, Larry dived to Juan's right as well. But at the last minute, Juan swerved left and let loose with the kick. Larry hit the dirt. The ball shot forward through the goal drums, easily passing Larry and landing several yards beyond him.

"He's awesome!" exclaimed Nick.

"Too bad he doesn't have a twin!" Sue and Lou shouted together.

"He couldn't have a twin," said Jeffrey. "He isn't *human*."

Larry, who was still on the ground, looked up. "He's the answer," he said.

"What was the question?" asked Evan.

"*How are we gonna win?*" asked Tak.

The kids nodded at one another and said, "Juan." But it was too late. Juan had already walked off the field and was heading home.

Drafting Juan

"Hey, he's getting away!" shouted Nick.

Nick and the other kids took off after Juan, who was halfway down the road by this time.

"Wait up!" Sue and Lou called out.

"We need to talk to you!" added Jeffrey.

Juan stopped and turned around. "Yeah?" he said with surprise.

"Where'd you learn to play like that?" asked Nick.

"In El Paso," shrugged Juan. "Everybody plays there."

"Well, you gotta play with us here," begged Evan.

Juan shook his head no.

"C'mon," insisted Sophia. "We need you. You're so good!"

"No," Juan said flatly.

"Hey, just play with us during recess," suggested Jeffrey.

"Please," pleaded Polly. "When Newt's not around

we don't have enough players."

Juan thought about the suggestion. He wanted to play soccer with the kids.

Kate put the ball on the ground and kicked it to Juan. "C'mon," she challenged. "You're on my team."

Juan smiled and happily followed Kate and the others back onto the playing field. Because of Juan, Kate's team won, 6–0.

"So you were holding out on us?" Anna asked Juan when the game was over.

"It's just a game," said Juan modestly.

"Not the way you play it," said Nick.

"Wait till we go to Austin," Jeffrey said eagerly. "We're gonna kick butt all the way to Pizza Hut!"

Suddenly Juan's happy expression faded. "I can play at recess," he told everyone. "But I can't go to Austin."

The kids were stunned.

"What'd'ya mean?" asked Kate.

"I can't," Juan said flatly. "Sorry."

"I don't get it," said Jeffrey.

"It's a family thing," Juan tried to explain. But he could see from their expressions that the kids didn't understand. His mother would never let him go to Austin to play in the tournament. But if he played only at school, she might never have to know.

••••• •••••

After school the kids held a special meeting. They needed a plan to persuade Juan's mother to let him play in Saturday's upcoming game. It was decided that the direct approach was best, so as soon as evening fell they all went over to the trailer park.

Kate knocked on the Moraleses' door.

"Are you Juan's mother?" Kate asked when the door opened.

Mrs. Morales nodded.

"We gotta talk to you," said Nick.

Mrs. Morales led the kids into the small trailer. Juan sat down next to his mother and the kids explained to Mrs. Morales why they had come.

Mrs. Morales shook her head. "I don't want Juan going off by himself to the city," she said.

"He's not by himself," said Polly. "We all go."

"He'd probably do better without us, Mrs. Morales," said Larry. "But it's a team sport."

"Austin's really not that far," added Tak.

"You could come," Jeffrey suggested. "My mom's gonna go this time."

"I can't," said Mrs. Morales. "I work during the day."

"We'll look out for him, ma'am," said Newt. "We promise."

Mrs. Morales looked at Juan. He looked at her. She knew he wanted more than anything to play soccer with his classmates. In so many towns since they'd come to this country, they had been made to feel different, like outsiders. These kids from Elma were making Juan feel as if he were a part of their group, as if he belonged.

She didn't want to stand in the way of that.

••••• •••••

That Saturday morning a string of cars from Elma pulled into the parking lot at Austin High. This time, not only were Tom and Anna there, but some of the kids' parents had come along as well. The kids, now dressed in green T-shirts, piled out of the cars. Juan Morales got out and surveyed their opponents.

They were called the Terminators, and they looked like they could definitely terminate the kids from Elma.

Tom opened the trunk of his car and pulled out a large box filled with cardboard strips, egg cartons, bubble wrap, and masking tape.

"My Aunt Burr used to say that anything you need in life can probably be made with masking tape or spit," he told Anna as she helped him lift the box out of the trunk.

"So what are we making?" Anna asked, looking at the odd materials.

"Shin guards," replied Tom.

Tom outfitted each one of the kids with shin guards made out of the cardboard and bubble wrap.

When the referee blew the start-up whistle, the Big Green took their positions on the field, across from the Terminators. The Terminators snickered and giggled when they saw the ragtag team from Elma.

The referee placed the ball at Juan's feet and then blew his whistle. Juan kicked the ball to Kate, who was playing left forward. As they had practiced in Elma, Kate kicked the ball right back to Juan, who began dribbling it into Terminator territory and toward the goal net. Jeffrey, playing the right, spread out and crossed the center line as well.

Juan passed the ball to Jeffrey, who trapped it and

then continued across the field. After he had dribbled the ball a few feet, he passed it back to Juan.

The Terminators saw that Juan was the Big Green's star player. They instinctively concentrated on defending against him, triple teaming him at one point.

But Juan was too nimble. He kicked the ball and crossed it to Tak.

"Shoot!" Anna and Tom urged Tak from the sideline. "Kick it in, Tak!"

But Tak hesitated, afraid. He wasn't sure what to do. He clumsily kicked the ball back toward Juan. The ball was quickly intercepted by a Terminator middleman.

The Terminator drove the ball down the field and dribbled it into Big Green territory. None of the kids from Elma moved to block him. When the Terminator reached the far end of the field, he easily kicked the ball past Larry and into the goal net.

Juan watched the play in amazement. Then he turned to Tak.

"What's wrong with you?!" he shouted angrily. "You were wide open!"

Tak looked like he was about to cry.

Kate Scores

Although the Big Green tried hard, they just couldn't seem to play as a team. Whenever anyone got control of the ball, it was immediately passed to Juan. No sooner would he get the ball than Juan found himself triple-played by Terminators. They wanted to keep him away from the goal net.

By the middle of the second half, the score was 6–0, Terminators.

A Terminator headed toward Larry for the seventh goal.

Larry panicked. His heart was beating rapidly. Sweat was pouring down his face and into his eyes. Suddenly the oncoming Terminator changed into a huge Arnold Schwarzenegger look-alike—complete with leather jacket and motorcycle! A *real* Terminator!

Larry covered his eyes and dove to the ground. When he opened his eyes, Arnold Schwarzenegger was gone. And the Terminator middleman had scored a point.

"You OK?" Evan asked, running over to Larry.

Larry pulled Evan over to the side. "Can I tell you a secret?" he asked. Evan nodded. "When I get really afraid they change into bad guys. I mean they *really* change."

Evan looked at his friend. "You're a pretty complicated guy," he told Larry doubtfully.

Just then, the ref blew his whistle, signaling the end of the third quarter. The kids ran over to Tom and Anna on the sidelines.

"No one's passing to me," complained Polly.

"You just lose the ball," Nick said accusingly.

"Well, *too* many people are passing to me!" exclaimed Juan angrily.

"Quiet down," Tom told the kids. "Listen to me."

"Why should we listen to you?" asked Jeffrey.

"Because I'm your coach," replied Tom.

"No," said Larry. "You're just here 'cause you're after our coach."

"Look," began Tom. "I'm here, midgets. That should be enough."

Anna was getting dismayed. "This is wrong!" she interrupted. "We don't fight with each other. On the field or off. That is not what we talked about when we spoke of teamwork." Then she turned to Tom and said, "And quit calling them midgets!"

"Yeah!" said Evan.

Tom paused. "OK," he said. "She's right. Now, listen up. Juan can't do everything. You've got to pass to each other."

“But he’s the only one who’s any good,” said Tak.

“Right now playing as a team is more important than winning,” said Tom.

“And when we can play as a team, maybe we will be able to win,” added Anna.

“Now, you’ve got ten minutes left,” said Tom. “Support each other! If they put three guys on Juan, that means two of you are open. Take advantage of it.”

When the game resumed, the Terminators quickly got control of the ball and began charging toward the Big Green’s net. A Terminator took a shot, but Larry stopped the ball, landing on it with his whole body. Then he kicked the ball across the field to Juan.

“Juan, keep it outta here!” Larry shouted.

Juan took command of the ball and charged across the center line into Terminator territory. Tak and Kate were running parallel to him.

Juan worked his way toward the Terminator’s goal net. He saw Kate and passed the ball to her. She instantly passed the ball back to him. Juan stared at her. She was centered in front of the net and was in a better position to score. He passed the ball to her again.

“Talk about being in the wrong place at the wrong time,” Kate said to herself as the ball reached her.

“Kate!” shouted Juan. “Shoot!!!”

Kate hesitated, uncertain. Then she booted the ball hard. The ball sailed past the Terminator goalie.

The Big Green team leaped and cheered.

Tom, Anna, and the parents charged onto the field

and converged upon Kate with smiles.

"You scored!" Juan said, running up to Kate.

"I did?" asked Kate with surprise. It seemed like a dream to her.

"You did!" said Juan.

"I did," realized Kate. "I did! I did!"

Then, without thinking, she put her arms around Juan and gave him a big hug. Juan, also without thinking, hugged her back.

As soon as they realized what they were doing, they pulled apart, their faces red with embarrassment.

Team Spirit

That evening, Kate returned home tired and dirty from the day's game. She was feeling good, despite the fact that the Big Green had lost to the Terminators 16-3.

But Kate's heart sank when she entered the house. Ed was lying on the couch. Drunk, as usual.

"You're late," said Ed.

"We stopped at Pizza Hut after the game," Kate explained. "I scored a point."

Ed was silent. Kate waited for a reaction but didn't get one. She started for her room.

"Ya win?" Ed asked as she started up the stairs.

"No," she said, and went into her room and closed the door. But moments later she opened the door and yelled, "Next time we'll win!"

••••• •••••

It was drizzling the next day, but the rain hadn't stopped the Big Green from meeting for soccer practice in the school yard. A game was scheduled for the following Saturday, and this time the kids wanted to be ready for it. Even their parents had come out to the practice field to cheer them on.

"That's enough for today!" Anna shouted as soon as it began to rain harder. But the kids ignored her and kept practicing.

"That's it!" shouted Tom. "Practice is over!"

"It's not over for us!" shouted Nick. Then he passed the ball to Sophia.

Anna and Tom ran onto the field and tried to get the ball away from Sophia, but she passed it to Juan. Once Juan had the ball, he passed it to Evan.

Cookie Dunk turned to the other parents and said, "We'd better help them out. Those kids'll never give up the ball."

Cookie ran onto the field and tried to get the ball away from one of the kids. Before he knew it he was scrimmaging with them.

"Dad!" shouted Larry from the goal area. "What are you doing?"

"I'm playing soccer!" Cookie answered gleefully.

Cookie was having so much fun the other parents decided to join in. Suddenly a game was being played: parents against the kids. Soon everybody was wet and muddy. Even Kate really got into it, and everybody noticed how good she was. And nobody could remember the last time they had this much fun in Elma.

"What have you done to us?" Tom asked Anna as they both tried to cover Nick, who had the ball.

"I didn't do anything," Anna said breathlessly.

"Yes, you did," insisted Tom, pointing to all the players. "You did this."

"Don't be silly," said Anna.

Suddenly Tom stopped playing and allowed Nick to get away with the ball. Anna stopped when she saw that Tom had a serious expression on his face.

"You've done something to me," Tom told Anna earnestly. "I feel like I was asleep, and when I met you I finally woke up."

"Go back to sleep," Anna joked. But then she smiled warmly at Tom.

••••• •••••

The feeling in Elma had changed in the weeks since Anna's kids joined the soccer league. Not only were the kids excited about something, but the adults were as well.

Bomma Cole dyed white cotton soccer jerseys green. Anna cut some position numbers out of felt and sewed them on the jerseys. . . .

Newt, Evan, and Tak got some cows to "mow" the playing field. Sue and Lou, with the help of Jeffrey and Nick, transformed an old fishing net into a goal net. Now the kids had real practice goals instead of metal drums. . . .

Jeffrey's dad, Albert, and Newt's mom, Connie, looked through a sports-equipment catalog with Tom and chipped in to buy some *real* shin guards, *clean* sneakers, and *brand-new* soccer balls. . . .

Cookie placed a hand-painted sign in the window of The Office that read: GO BIG GREEN. . . .

And go they did. The kids practiced every day during recess and after school. On some mornings they even got to the school yard early to get in some practice before the bell rang.

They were determined to be ready for that next match in Austin.

Feeling Special

That Saturday, Larry watched as the opposing team, the Ninjas, charged across the Austin soccer field toward him.

On the outside he felt good in his new Big Green uniform, shin guards, and sneakers. But on the inside he was scared.

It was happening again. As they drew closer, the Ninjas seemed to change right before his eyes. Their rugby shirts and shorts changed into sleek black ninja warrior costumes. Their flailing arms now waved long, gleaming swords.

"This is a real problem," groaned Larry as he shut his eyes and dove blindly for the ball.

Thump! Larry opened his eyes. He had blocked it! Then he heard his father cheer from the sideline, "Way to go, Larry!"

Larry sighed with relief. The real ninjas had changed back to regular kids. Not only that, but

Evan had gotten control of the ball and was now dribbling with his foot toward the center line! Then he booted the ball, sending it several yards to Juan, who was already running to intercept it. Juan trapped the ball with his instep, dribbled it a few feet, and then spiked it toward the Ninjas' goal and scored.

The kids jumped in celebration. The parents hugged one another. Anna and Tom slapped each other in a high five.

The Big Green played better and better soccer in the weeks that followed. In game four, against the Zombies, they won 4–1. In game five they played the Gladiators and won 6–2.

The kids felt great. They were filled with new enthusiasm. And they had Anna to thank for it all. One day they gathered early in their classroom and decorated the blackboard with paintings, pictures, and two maps: one of Texas, the other of England.

"Here she comes!" Polly shouted to the kids. She was watching through the window as Anna approached. The kids scurried into their seats just as she entered the room.

"We figured out what makes us special," Larry said as Anna reached her desk.

"I can see that," said Anna, noticing the newly decorated blackboard.

"It's not all the stuff we put up, ma'am," said Tak.

Then Kate stood up. "It's you."

Anna looked at Kate. She was so happy, she almost started to cry. Then she pulled a copy of the *Austin Gazette* out from her lesson-plan book, spread it open, and slapped it between the two maps on the blackboard with a piece of scotch tape.

A headline across the newspaper read: DISTRICT SOCCER CHAMPIONSHIPS SET DIVISION #3 FINALS—ELMA BIG GREEN TO FACE OFF AGAINST AUSTIN KNIGHTS.

The kids cheered. They were set for a rematch. The Knights had clobbered them their first time out.

But this time the Big Green would be ready for them.

Huffer's Plan

They were standing on the Big Green, all freshly mowed and cleaned and set up for soccer, when a sleek Cadillac pulled up to the school yard and Jay Huffer got out.

"Look who's here," said Kate.

"I remember him," said Jeffrey.

"I'll *always* remember him," said Larry.

Anna added, "It's the *pinhead*."

"Anna," said Tom, gently nudging her in the ribs with his elbow, "that's *our* little name for him, OK?"

"Place hasn't changed," Jay said. "You can say that much."

"You haven't, either," Tom said. "Makes it even."

Jay noticed Juan standing among the kids. "See you dug up a ringer," he said.

"He's one of Anna's students," explained Tom.

"What a twist of fate," said Jay. "Some real talent finally back in the area."

"Look," Tom began, "I know we never liked each other as kids, but—"

"We couldn't stand each other as kids," corrected Jay. "Once my team beats you on Saturday, it'll only get worse."

"It can't get worse," said Tom.

"And you're not going to beat us on Saturday," added Anna.

Jay smirked. "You two make quite a team," he said.

"Thanks," Anna and Tom said together.

"I didn't come to chat," Jay said in a serious tone of voice. "I came to give the team the once-over."

Anna didn't want the Knights' coach watching her kids practice. "It would be great for you to watch, but . . . ," began Anna, then she blew her whistle and shouted to the kids, "PRACTICE IS OVER!"

The kids stopped playing and stared at Jay.

"I've seen enough," he said. "Have 'em ready on Saturday. Maybe it'll be a better game than last time."

Then he turned around and returned to his car. He didn't want them to see how worried he was.

"What a pinhead," Anna and Tom said to each other as they watched Huffer drive off.

••••• •••••

Angry and shaken, Jay Huffer stopped in front of The Office. He needed a drink.

"Well, if it isn't Jay Huffer in from the big city," said Cookie when Jay entered. A quick glance at the bar made Jay even angrier: photos of the kids of the

Big Green were everywhere. Cookie was wearing a green shirt. Even the beer was green.

"A mini-mall is a big city compared to this place," Jay said snidely as he approached the bar. "Gimme a double scotch."

"Things are that good?" Ed asked Jay from his stool.

"It's one of those days," Jay shrugged.

"What ya doing for a living nowadays, Jay?" asked Cookie as he placed a rocks glass of scotch in front of Huffer.

"I'm an auditor for the tax department," answered Jay. "And I'm darned good at it." He took another look at the photos on the wall. "So, somehow you all got yourself a good soccer team," he said.

"They're winners," said Cookie. "This town had gotten out of the habit of winning. It feels good."

"Hard to believe the Mexican kid is the star," Ed growled as he took another sip of green beer.

"Juan is incredible," Cookie told Ed. "And Kate's darn good, too. You oughta watch her play."

"I got better things to do," Ed said bitterly.

"Just my luck, someone who could play would move here," said Jay as he took a sip of his drink.

"Yeah," agreed Ed. "If people would stay put, it would change things. I'm sick of solving everyone else's problems."

Jay's eyes narrowed as he focused on the photo of Juan that was pinned over the bar. "I wonder if they're legal?" he asked half-aloud.

"Probably not," said Ed. "Most foreigners aren't."

Ed's comment gave Jay an idea. If Juan Morales

were an illegal alien, he couldn't be in the soccer league. In fact, neither he nor his mother would be allowed in the United States. And without Juan, the Big Green would stand no chance against the Knights. No chance at all.

Jay bought Ed some more beers and asked questions about Juan. He made Ed take him past Juan's trailer. Then Jay called the sheriff's office and asked to speak to the chief of police. Chief Bishop got on the phone.

Without giving his name, Jay told the chief that the Moraleses were illegal immigrants and that they were living in a trailer park near the outskirts of Elma.

Good-bye, Juan

The next morning, Tom pulled up in front of Marbelly Morales's trailer, but he didn't get out of his car. He didn't want to believe that what Chief Bishop told him earlier that morning was true. The chief had received an anonymous tip that the Moraleses may be illegals.

After a few minutes Tom got out and knocked on the door. When Mrs. Morales answered she said, "Hey Tom, is everything OK?"

Tom replied, "You tell me," and told her about the anonymous phone call.

Once inside the trailer, Tom said he could help the Moraleses.

"And you can hurt me," said Mrs. Morales, "you're the law."

"Right now I'm not," said Tom reassuringly.

"Ten minutes from now you will be," replied Mrs. Morales.

Juan appeared at the bedroom door. He was dressed for school, but he had heard everything.

"Mom," he said, "tell him."

Mrs. Morales paused. She had no choice but to tell Tom the truth.

"I've been in America for fourteen years," she told Tom. "But Juan was born in El Paso. He's a citizen. They had amnesty eight years ago, but I didn't apply. I'd gone back to El Salvador to see my parents. You are supposed to have stayed in this country the whole time."

"Do the people you work for now know you're illegal?" asked Tom.

"I bought a fake social security card in San Antonio five years ago," said Mrs. Morales. "I pay taxes and social security under that name." She looked at Juan. "I have an American son. But I can be deported. Sent back. Just like that."

Tom looked at Mrs. Morales helplessly. She had started to cry.

••••• •••••

"Are you sure she was crying?" Anna asked Kate.

"Yes," replied Kate. "She was really upset."

Kate had told everyone in the classroom what she'd seen that morning. She'd been on her way to school, walking past the trailer park as she usually did, when she saw Tom's police car parked in front of Juan's trailer. Suspecting something was up, she had ducked behind a tree and watched as Tom and Mrs. Morales emerged from the trailer.

"Let's get over there!" Kate urged Anna.

"No," replied Anna. "School starts in ten minutes.

I'm sure Juan will be here, and we'll make sure everything's OK."

"But everything's *not* OK!" insisted Kate. "That's what I'm telling you!"

"You're overreacting," Anna firmly told Kate. "Sit down."

Kate huffed and went to her desk.

"You're wrong," she said sullenly. "You'll see."

Anna began teaching the first lesson of the day. Later, Juan still hadn't arrived for school.

"Maybe he's got a cold or something," said Polly.

"He's not sick!" said Kate.

Anna was beginning to worry. At recess she went to the school office to call Juan's mother. When there was no answer, she called Tom.

The kids waited in the school yard while Anna was in the office. But they were becoming impatient.

"I'm going to his house," Kate told the others.

"But we're not allowed to leave school," warned Polly.

Kate didn't care what Polly said. She ran out of the school yard and headed straight for the trailer park.

She wasn't alone. The rest of the Big Green followed right behind her. When they got to the trailer park, they knew at once that Juan and his mother were gone. Their car was nowhere to be found, and their trailer looked empty.

"We just lost our center forward!" said Nick.

"We also just lost our *friend*, too," Sophia said.

Red-faced, Nick nodded in agreement.

Larry said, "And now we're busted."

Everybody looked toward the road. Tom was pulling up in his patrol car. And Anna was with him.

"What are you kids doing here?" asked Anna, getting out.

"They're gone!" said Kate. "We can see inside. Their stuff's all gone!"

Tom glanced through the window of the trailer. "She panicked," he said.

"I told you," said Kate. Then she threw a scornful look at Tom and said, "*You* did it! It's your fault! I saw you here!"

And with that, Kate took off down the road at a run.

KATE'S VOW

Kate was out of breath by the time she got home and slammed the door behind her. She had run all the way from the trailer park.

Her father, heaped on the couch, stirred when he heard her come in.

"What got into *you*?" he asked Kate.

"Juan's gone," Kate told him.

"The Mexi kid?"

Kate's face hardened. "Don't call him that!" she shouted at her father. "Don't you *ever* call him that!"

"I didn't mean nothing by it," Ed said, stunned that Kate was so angry.

Kate stared at her father. "Yeah, you did," she told him accusingly.

"What's gotten into you?" asked Ed.

"As soon as I'm old enough, I'm outta here," Kate told him. "Nobody in their right mind would stay in this town!"

"Now wait a minute—"

"Don't worry," interrupted Kate. "You'll never know I'm gone. You don't even know I'm here right now!"

She walked back out the front door, slamming it behind her. Then she ran all the way to the old granary, climbed up to her secret room, and looked at all her special things. She hated everything she saw. She pulled out her pocketknife and began slashing at everything in sight: the pictures on the walls, the throw pillows, everything. When she was done she found that she didn't feel any better. She collapsed on the floor and cried.

Kate didn't want to go home, so she went for a walk into town.

"Been looking for you," came a voice from out of nowhere. Kate swerved around, startled. Anna was standing behind her.

"Small town," Kate said flatly. "Not a lot of places to look."

"I found quite a few," said Anna. Anna explained to Kate why the Moraleses had left Elma. "Tom had no idea they were going to leave," Anna continued. "He was trying to help them. A lot of people would have tried to help them. But they got scared."

"They didn't even say good-bye," Kate said bitterly.

"I'm sorry."

"That's how you know they aren't coming back," said Kate. "People only say good-bye when they plan on saying hello again. It's a rule."

Anna put her arms around Kate's shoulder,

giving her a gentle hug. “The other kids don’t know if they want to play tomorrow.” Then she added, “They think maybe we should forfeit.”

“What do you think?” asked Kate.

“I think Juan would want you to do well,” replied Anna. “In school *and* in soccer.”

“He wouldn’t want me to do well,” Kate said. “He’d want me to *win*.”

Return to Austin

The next morning, everyone in town gathered in front of The Office to see the Big Green off to their long-awaited match in Austin.

After a while, Anna and Bomma Cole pulled up in Anna's red convertible. Everyone gathered around as they got out of the car, opened the trunk, and pulled out a box. Anna sliced open the box and pulled out a set of clean and neatly wrapped green uniforms. Each shirt had a different number on it and the name *Adidas* sewn onto the back. They were *real* uniforms!

"Where'd they come from?" Sue and Lou asked as they took their new uniforms from Anna.

"Everyone chipped in," explained Anna. "As a surprise."

"Hey, where's the sheriff?" asked Larry. Tom was nowhere to be seen, and it was almost time to go.

“He was out all night looking for Juan and his mother,” said Anna.

“Did he find them?” asked Sophia.

“No. But he's going to meet us in Austin later.”

“Where's Kate?” asked Cookie Dunk. Everyone looked around. Kate wasn't there either.

“If she doesn't show up, we forfeit!” exclaimed Larry. “It's bad enough playing without Juan!”

Just then, Kate came running down the street, surprising everyone.

“What are you all staring at?” Kate asked. “Let's get going. We need time to warm up!”

The kids, their parents, Anna, and just about everybody else in town piled into their cars and headed to Austin.

A little more than an hour later, the caravan of cars from Elma reached Austin. A pregame parade was going on around Austin Stadium that day. The Austin Knights drove by in expensive convertibles, their fans cheering them on as they went.

“We look like a buncha hicks compared to the Knights,” said Polly's mother as she drove along the parade route in her flatbed truck.

“Hate to break it to ya, babe,” said Cookie, who was sitting beside her. “But we *are* a bunch of hicks.”

After a while, the two teams reached the stadium and took to the field. The Knights began their warm-ups.

“They don't look so hot,” Kate said aloud.

“They scare me,” said Larry.

“Visualize a victory,” suggested Tak.

"I'd rather visualize a pizza," replied Larry.

Anna walked over and waved the kids into a huddle.

"No matter how you do out there," she told them, "I want you kids to know that we're proud of you. Warm up, you guys!"

The kids ran onto the field and began kicking a ball around. The Knights stopped practicing to watch. This time they didn't laugh. The kids from Elma had gotten better since the last time they played them. *Much* better.

"Where's the coach?" Jay Huffer said as he approached Anna on the sidelines.

"I'm the coach," replied Anna.

"I mean Palmer," said Jay.

"He'll be here."

Jay glanced out on the field, searching for Juan Morales. He wasn't there.

"Where's your star player?" he asked, secretly smiling to himself.

"Everyone on our team is a star," Anna shot back sharply.

"We'll see about that," Jay said pompously. "We got a tradition around these parts. Coaches make wagers before the game."

"What are we betting for?" asked Anna.

"I'd hate to take your money," answered Jay. "But I wouldn't say no to a kiss."

"Deal," Anna said devilishly. "But if we win you kiss our mascot." She pointed to Ernie the goat, who was munching on a pile of garbage.

Upset, Jay shouted to his team, "You better not lose!"

Just then, the referee's whistle blew. The ref had just placed the ball at Kate's feet. The game had begun.

Kate kicked the ball to her right, passing it to Nick. Nick trapped the ball with his instep and immediately passed it back to Kate. At once, the Knights charged at her.

Kate swerved and sliced the ball to Jeffrey with a clumsy but effective banana kick. Her spirits soared. It wasn't the best kick in the world, but it worked.

"Hey, my kid's good!" exclaimed one of the parents on the sidelines. The other parents turned around, surprised to see that Kate's father, Ed, had come along after all. And he was wearing a clean shirt, too.

"Look who showed up," said Cookie, giving Ed a friendly pat on the back.

Back on the field, Jeffrey was too slow. Jay Huffler, Jr., a Knight forward, intercepted the ball Kate had just passed. His teammates covered him, and now they drove the ball across Big Green territory toward the goal. When he was close enough, he forward kicked the ball past Larry and scored.

Anna could see the disappointment on the kids' faces.

"That's OK!" she shouted reassuringly. "That's all right. You're doing great!"

But deep down she knew the Big Green was in trouble. Without Juan she didn't know if they stood a chance. She looked around, then at her watch.

Where was Tom? she wondered.

Surprise Kick

"Tom will be here any minute," Anna told the kids at halftime. They had gathered at the sidelines and were gulping down water. But the kids were not hopeful. The game was half over and the score was 2–0, Knights.

"If he's not here any minute, why bother?" asked Sophia.

"You guys are doing great," said Anna. She was trying her best to sound encouraging.

"Two to zero," Nick said with disappointment.

"It's better than seventeen to zero," said Kate.

"Point well-taken," said Evan.

"Hey," said Newt with a smile on his face. "I'm havin' fun!"

"We know," Nick said with a groan. "Nobody ever asks you to do anything."

When the game resumed, the Knights pummeled the Big Green mercilessly. With ten minutes left in the game, Jay Junior sneered at Kate from his forward-center position.

"You're ten minutes from curtains," Jay Junior taunted.

"Maybe," said Kate. "But you're a whole lifetime from having a brain."

The ref tossed the ball to Jay Junior and was just about to blow the starting whistle when one of the Elma parents shouted, "Look!"

Tom Palmer's patrol car had just pulled up to the field. The sheriff climbed out. And Mrs. Morales and Juan were with him.

The kids of the Big Green leaped for joy and ran to meet Juan.

"You're back!" said Kate.

"Yeah," said Juan, glancing over at the Knights. "I came to beat these guys!"

Anna approached Tom. "What happened?" she asked.

"I found them outside of Alvin," replied Tom.

"It looked like a good place to hide," added Mrs. Morales. "But Tom's got a better plan than running for the rest of my life."

"We've already got her a lawyer," said Tom.

"And Tom's going to be my sponsor," added Mrs. Morales.

Tom shrugged. "If I'm going to spend my life in a little town, I gotta get good people there with me."

"So you made it, coach!" Jay Huffer shouted to Tom from across the field.

"I was just bringing the last member of our team," Tom shouted back.

"Everyone *qualified* to be here deserves to be here," Jay shot back.

"They all qualify," replied Tom. He smiled at Mrs. Morales and added, "and so do their families."

By now, the kids had returned to the field. Juan took his position as center forward, and Jeffrey moved to the middle line.

"You didn't even say good-bye," Kate said to Juan as they took their positions beside each other.

"Don't be mad," said Juan. "I wanted to."

"I can't believe you're here," Kate said with a smile. "If you ever leave again, say good-bye."

"If I ever leave again," Juan told her, "I'm taking you with me."

The ref threw the ball back onto the field and blew his whistle.

Juan charged the ball and passed it to Kate. It was a short pass that Kate trapped firmly. Then she began to dribble the ball toward the Knights' goal. A Knight winger tried to steal the ball, but Kate could see that Juan was a few yards away, heading for the goal himself. She lunged to the left, and the Knight's winger went with her. Then she faked him out and lunged back to the right. She brought her leg back and flicked the ball to Juan, who sent it into the goal net.

Juan and Kate met each other with victorious high fives.

Anna, Tom, and the parents cheered from the sidelines.

The score was now 2–1.

"One goal," Anna said.

"One goal," repeated Tom. "One goal and we tie!"

Once again the ref blew his whistle, and once again Juan charged the soccer ball and began driving it across Knight territory and toward the goal.

That's when Jay Huffer, Jr., ran to block Juan. Their legs mingled in an intense effort for control of the ball. Then Juan felt Jay Junior's shin against his. Jay Junior pulled his leg across Juan's, and Juan went tumbling, face downward, to the ground.

Goal Play

It was an intentional trip up and Juan knew it. He rose to his feet just in time to see Jay Huffer, Jr., drive the ball across the center line and kick it straight toward the Big Green net.

That's when Polly plowed in front of the ball and blocked it with her chest. It was a perfect save.

Jay Huffer, Sr., screamed so loud he could be heard clear across the field. "What's *wrong* with you guys?!" he shouted at the Knights. "*They're* controlling the ball! You're not trying hard enough!"

"You can shout all you want, but I don't think it's gonna help," one of the Knights yelled back at their coach.

"You're gonna be beaten by a bunch of *girls!*" Jay screamed, his face red with rage.

"Hey, give us a break," another Knight shouted. "We're doing our best."

But the Knight's best was not good enough for

their coach. He pulled the two players who had yelled back at him out of the game and replaced them with two subs. There were only two minutes left in the game, and Jay Huffer wasn't going to risk a tie.

The ref blew the whistle. As soon as he heard that sound, Juan got possession of the ball and moved up the field toward the Knights' net. The Knights crowded on Juan and blocked his path. Juan had seen them coming, though. He knew there was no way the Knights were going to let him tie the game easily. He scanned the field for an open player and found Kate running on the outside. He kicked the ball toward her just before three Knights surrounded him.

Kate received the ball effortlessly. Now the Knights went after *her*. That gave Juan the freedom he needed to outrun the three guards and sprint toward the net.

Kate saw him and passed the ball back to him before the Knights could reach her. It was a clear, straight pass that flew through the air, hit the ground and rolled straight to Juan's feet. Juan kicked the ball toward the net.

The Knights' goalie ran to meet the ball. He leaped into the air and deflected it with the tip of his fingers. He couldn't control it, though, and it went back toward the field.

Tak realized that the ball was flying straight toward him. He knew that there was only one way to make the play. He lowered his head and smashed the ball directly into the net. GOAL!

The ref blew his whistle. The game was over! The kids cheered, and their fans screamed with excitement.

They had tied the game!

The Tiebreaker

"The regulation play has resulted in a tie!" announced the referee. "We will go into a shoot-out!"

The Big Green gathered around Anna as Tom explained what happens in a tied game.

"Five players from each team will go out onto the field. And you will each take a shot against the goalie."

"Let Juan kick five times," Polly suggested.

"Each player can only kick once," Anna explained.

Tom told Juan to go first. He would be followed by Kate, Nick, and Sophia. But they still needed someone to shoot last.

"Any volunteers for the last position?" asked Tom. "Jeffrey?"

"My kick's no good," replied Jeffrey. "Don't make me do it."

"Evan?" asked Anna.

"Don'tcha remember I swallowed a whole pencil

last year?" asked Evan. "I could be dying right now. I can't do it. I could choke. Literally."

"No way," said Sue and Lou when Anna looked at them pleadingly. Then she asked Tak if he'd like to take the last position.

"I already did my thing," Tak said. "I feel like a hero. Don't take it away from me! How 'bout Polly?"

"I would," said Polly. "Really. But I have a stomachache. And a fever. Came on real sudden."

It seemed as if nobody wanted to take last position.

Just then, Newt raised his hand. "I'll do it," he said.

Everyone stared at Newt. Nobody had thought to ask him.

"I don't think so," said Larry.

"Why?" asked Newt. "I got a great kick. And I'm not afraid."

Tom and Anna exchanged looks. "What do you think?" Anna asked Tom.

"I'm little," said Newt. "I'm low to the ground. I got power. I got the moves. I'm your man!"

"In soccer, size isn't important," said Anna.

"C'mon," Newt insisted. "I can boot. And I got nerves of steel."

Tom nodded. "You got the job, big guy," he told Newt.

Newt leaped up and down. "Wow!" he exclaimed. "You guys are the greatest!"

"Hey," Nick said, pointing his finger at Newt. "This may be the last time anybody lets you do anything—so don't mess it up."

Anna and Tom led Juan and the other shooters back toward the field.

"You guys played a great game," Tom told them. "If you miss your shots, run back to the circle with your head held high."

"That's right," said Anna. "You played brilliantly."

Tom added, "Now go get 'em."

The five shooters for the Big Green lined up in order at the center of the field. Beside them the five shooters for the Knights were already assembled.

Then the ref blew the whistle and the shoot-out began.

First up was a Knight. The ref placed the ball at his feet. The boy kicked, sending the ball straight toward the Big Green net. Larry lunged and tried to block the ball but missed. The ball went in, giving the Knights the winning edge.

Juan was up next. He looked at the ball, then at the Knights' net. Then he took a running kick. The ball flew inside the net. The Big Green was even once again!

The next Knight smashed the ball toward Larry. It was wide, and Larry was unable to block it. The Big Green were behind again.

Kate was up next. She kicked the ball, sending it straight into the Knights' net. It was 2–2.

The third Knight walked up to the next ball and kicked. The ball went flying high into the air. It was so high, it overshot the net.

The Big Green fans cheered from the sidelines.

Sophia was next. She stepped forward and shot the ball into the Knights' net.

The Big Green kids jumped for joy. They were now ahead by one point!

The fourth Knight was one of the biggest players the kids from Elma had ever seen. He looked as if he was all power. When he kicked the ball, it sailed across the field so fast it could hardly be seen.

Larry dived for the ground. There was no way he was going to even try and stop that ball.

The score was tied again.

Now it was Nick's turn to shoot. He lined up his shot with his eyes and then kicked. His kick was even and powerful. The ball flew straight toward the net, but the Knight goalie blocked it.

The score was 3–3, and each team had one player left.

The moment of truth had arrived.

The Big Score

"Time out!" called Larry. "Time out!"

He ran to the sidelines, freaked. Jay Huffer, Jr., was the next Knight to shoot. As he approached the ball, Larry's vision had begun to haze over. Once again Jay Junior looked like a *real* knight in *real* armor.

Larry was certain he couldn't defend the goal net against *that*.

"Make somebody else do it!" he pleaded with Tom and Anna. "I'm gonna choke. I'm gonna hafta close my eyes. He looks like a monster."

Tom and Anna kneeled beside Larry.

"We know you're scared," Tom told Larry in a gentle voice. "But you can't run away from it. You're the best goalie the team has."

"If you look at him and he's a monster," added Anna, "become part of the nightmare. Join it. Turn yourself into a monster and fight back."

Something about what Anna said seemed to make sense to Larry. He hadn't thought of turning the tables before. This he had to try. So he headed back to his position at the net.

Jay Junior was staring right at him with a nasty look in his eyes.

"Join the nightmare," Larry muttered to himself as if he was trying to make himself believe it. "Fight back."

By the time Larry reached the net, he felt like a different person. He was walking taller. His chest burst forward, and his shoulders spread themselves wide.

Jay Junior blinked. He noticed the change in Larry, too. Suddenly Larry took on a different form. He was wearing armor, like a real *Knight*. But the armor was made of leather, like a real *Terminator*. And a sword was in his hand, like a real *Ninja!*

Jay was scared, but he gritted his teeth and kicked the ball.

The ball sailed across the field. Larry saw it coming and dove into the air as if he had wings. He met the ball in midair as it slammed into his chest. It was a save!

The Big Green fans went wild with excitement. Then a hush came over the crowd. Anna and Tom braced themselves.

Little Newt had just walked up to the ball for the final kick.

Newt could feel everyone's eyes as they watched him. He knew that if he could score the point he'd win the game for Elma. He'd be a big hero. If he missed, no one would ever ask him to do anything again.

He knew he *had* to score.

Newt started to kick to the left, but changed his mind at the last minute and went right. Then, his footing gave way, and he began to slip backward. As he fell, his kicking foot made contact with the ball.

Newt landed on his back with a thud. He was sure that he had blown it. But when he looked up, the ball was sailing high in the air and heading straight for the Knights' goal net.

The Knights' goalie wobbled back and forth, trying to judge where the ball was going to come in. But he misjudged it.

The ball entered the net.

Newt had scored.

The Big Green had won!

The kids jumped all over one another, cheering in victory. The parents on the sidelines did the same. Anna and Tom went ballistic. Newt suddenly found himself being lifted off the ground and hoisted onto the shoulders of his teammates.

Ed ran onto the field and hugged Kate. Surprised, she gave her father a great big hug.

Across the field Jay Huffer snarled. Then he took one of the Knights' lances and pierced it into the soccer ball.

Anna turned to Tom and said, "Well, sheriff, we won! You know what that means . . ."

"Tell me," Tom said, smiling.

"It means we got Jay Huffer's goat!"

Tom wasn't sure what Anna meant by that. Then he saw that the kids were leading Ernie the goat across the field toward Jay Huffer.

And Jay Huffer leaned over and gave Ernie a big kiss on the snout.

Soon the original billboard with Tom and Jay was replaced by a billboard with a portrait of the kids proclaiming:

ELMA—HOME OF DISTRICT 34
JUNIOR SOCCER CHAMPIONS
THE BIG GREEN